Luna Loves World Book Day

Joseph Coelho   Fiona Lumbers

This book belongs to:

_____

I celebrated World Book Day 2021 with this gift
from my local bookseller and Andersen Press

#ShareAStory

Andersen Press

World Book Day

World Book Day's mission is to offer every child and young person the opportunity
to read and love books by giving you the chance to have a book of your own.
To find out more, and for loads of fun activities and recommendations
to help you keep reading visit **worldbookday.com**
World Book Day is a charity funded by publishers and booksellers in the UK and Ireland.
World Book Day is also made possible by generous sponsorship from
National Book Tokens and support from authors and illustrators.

Today is World Book Day
and Luna can't wait.
She has the whole day planned...
Dress-up and play as favourite book character.
Meet an author and an illustrator.
Buy a new book with a book token.

Mum drops Luna off at school.
All of the children are dressed as
their favourite book characters,
there are cats and dragons,
wizards and robots.

Luna is dressed as her
favourite book character:
a unicorn...
Check!

In assembly an author and an illustrator talk about their books. Their words and pictures

vibrate around the hall.

They read poems and stories
and get the whole school to draw.

Meet an author and
illustrator... Check!

At lunchtime Luna the Unicorn is adventuring through a magical forest,

and then shooting off into outer space.

But Luna's costume rips and she can't wear it anymore.

Dress-up and play as favourite book character... Uncheck!!!

In class, Luna is surrounded by
fairies and aliens, giants and tigers.

Luna misses her unicorn.

Dad meets Luna after school.
She is still sad about her unicorn.
"Don't worry," says Dad. "There's no need to feel low –
when there is book magic in a potato!"

"What's magic about a potato?" asks Luna.
"You'll see," says Dad.

At their local bookshop the children
are dressing potatoes as book characters.

Luna loves her little potato unicorn,
it prances around the shop
with all the other potato book characters.

The author and illustrator arrive!
Luna buys a book with her book token... Check!
And gets it signed by the author and illustrator... Check!

Whilst all the book characters play... Check!
Luna Loves World Book Day.

More **Luna** stories:

Coming soon **Luna Loves Dance**

Also available:

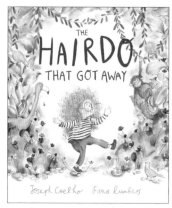

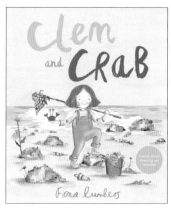